THAT PESKY TOASTER!

Ben Hillman

HYPERION BOOKS FOR CHILDREN
NEW YORK

To Goldie, my Grandma.
It's a book about *you*. So what's not to like?

Text and illustrations © 1995 by Ben Hillman.
All rights reserved. Printed in Singapore.
For more information address
Hyperion Books for Children, 114 Fifth Avenue, New York, New York 10011.

FIRST EDITION
1 3 5 7 9 10 8 6 4 2

Library of Congress Cataloging-in-Publication Data
Hillman, Ben.
That pesky toaster/Ben Hillman—1st ed.
p. cm.
Summary: Goldie's toaster doesn't work properly, creating a black hole instead of toast.
ISBN 0-7868-0033-X (trade)—ISBN 0-7868-2028-4 (lib. bdg.)
[1. Humorous stories. 2. Science fiction.] I. Title.
PZ7.H55955Th 1995
[E]—dc20 94–9831 CIP AC

The artwork for this book was prepared using mostly inks and dyes
with some oil paints and gouache on Strathmore regular finish illustration board.

This book is set in 18-point Caslon Open Face.

Design by Karen Palinko.

Such trouble my toaster's been giving Gus and me! I give it bread and she gobbles it up! Then, instead of toast, she spits out all kinds of who-knows-what! The toaster man said, "Goldie, this time for sure it is fixed. It will trouble you no more."

But the trouble was just beginning!...

There I was, making Gus his favorite bumbleberry pie, when all of a sudden I remembered my bread was burning up in the oven shed!

My bread! My bread! I forgot I was baking bread! I ran like mad to see it wasn't incinerated.

But just in time, I rescued my lovely loaves.

I sang to myself as I carried my newborns to the kitchen.

Now, mind you, not everyone can make a good slice of toast. You have to know what you're doing! First, carefully, you slice the bread...

...then you put the slices in the toaster. Any *other* toaster would make you toast. I held my breath and dropped the slices into the Unknown.

But did it give me toast? Not even close!

You think I need a galaxy running rampage through my house?
So I up with my broom to whack that thing's behind but good!

But the slippery weasel could dip and dodge like I don't know what!

I was jumpin' mad. I smacked that thing bad! I smacked it so hard, the varmint crashed into total astrophysical collapse!

A black hole in the house! That kind of rascally hole can swallow up anything! I need such a space-time singularity like a hole in the head.

And the nerve it had, to hide in Gus's favorite bumbleberry pie!

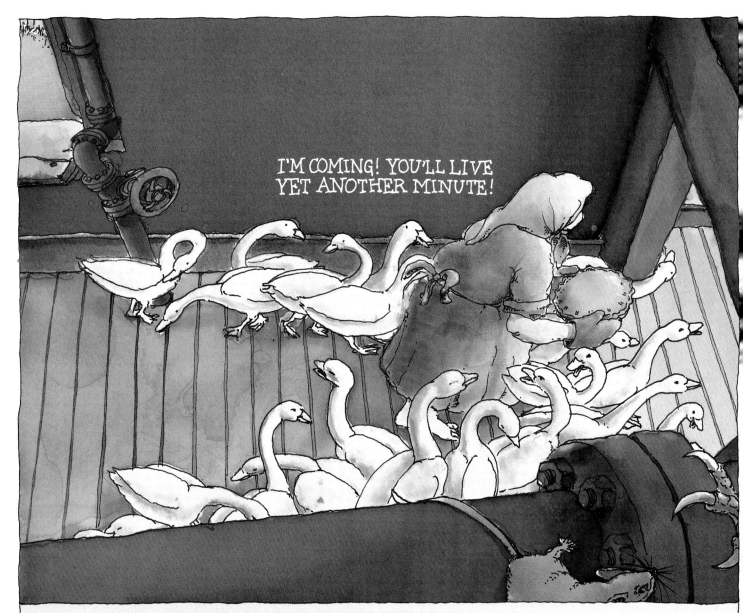

That hole just sat in my pie and wouldn't budge. And Gus started clamoring away for his dessert! I gave him eat. And crossed my fingers.

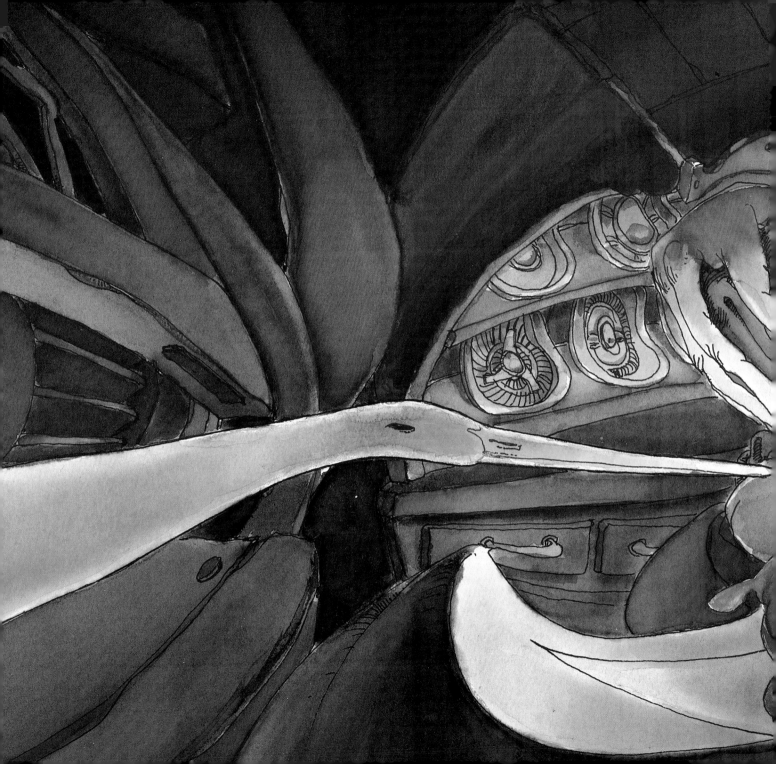

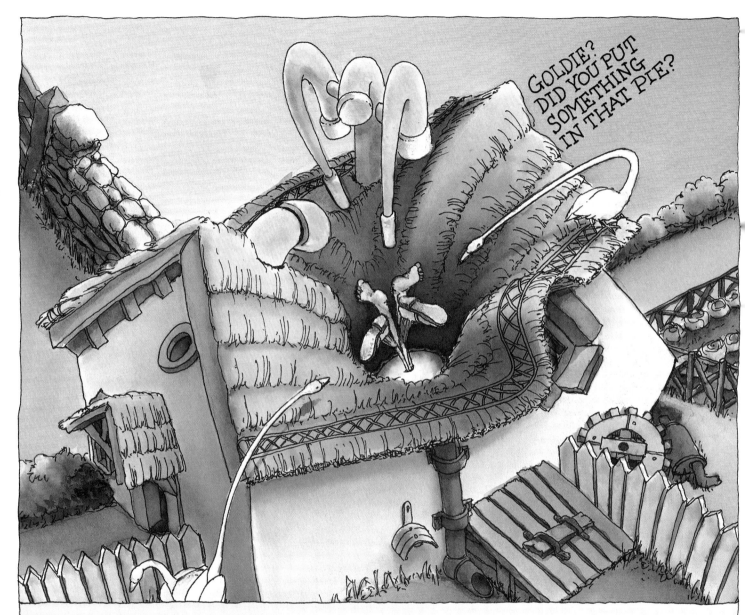

I just hope that black hole doesn't give Gus a tummy ache!

If my Gus gets sick from that pie, that toaster repair shop
is going to get a big piece of my mind...

I'll get my hands on that good-for-nothing fix-it man...

So much money he charges me for a toaster that pops up outer space!

The way Gus was chomping, that black-hole pie would soon be history.

I'm only hoping it shouldn't be indigestible!

But heaven be praised, nothing happened. My Gus, he slept like a log and a half.

Nothing happened, my neck! The universe was turned inside out!

Thank heaven that toaster has a two-year warranty!